Published by
Mind's Eye Publications
985 Deborah Avenue
Elgin, IL 60123-1918
mindseye.us.com

Cover Art by Paul "Mutartis" Boswell
Cover Design by Frank Coffman

MIND'S EYE

PUBLICATIONS

ISBN 978-1-7367114-0-8 Trade Paperback
$15.00 US

THE EXORCISED LYRIC

POEMS BY
STEVEN WITHROW
&
FRANK COFFMAN

THE EXORCISED LYRIC

POEMS BY
STEVEN WITHROW
&
FRANK COFFMAN

COVER AND
INTERIOR ILLUSTRATIONS BY
MUTARTIS BOSWELL

STEVEN WITHROW'S poems have appeared in *Spectral Realms, Asimov's Science Fiction, Dreams & Nightmares,* and *Epitaphs: The Journal of the New England Horror Writers.* His short poem, "The Sun Ships," from a collection of the same title, was nominated for a 2016 Rhysling Award from the Science Fiction & Fantasy Poetry Association. His most recent solo collection is *The Bedlam Philharmonic.* He lives in Falmouth, Massachusetts.

FRANK COFFMAN is a retired professor of college English, Creative Writing, and Journalism. His two collections of verse: *The Coven's Hornbook & Other Poems* and *Black Flames & Gleaming Shadows* have each received consideration for the Stoker Award from The Horror Writer's Association. He is also a member of the Science Fiction & Fantasy Poetry Association, and founded the Weird Poets Society Facebook group. He has published both speculative verse and short fiction in a variety of journals, magazines, and anthologies. He lives in Elgin, Illinois.

Cover Art, Frontispiece, and
Interior Illustrations by
Mutartis Boswell

Dedications

For Marin and Sunny
—S.W.

To my wife, Connie,
for her Love, Patience, and Support
—F.C.

Illustrations by
Mutartis Boswell

POET'S PREFACE
BY FRANK COFFMAN

This collection of verse by my friend, fellow poet, and "partner in rhyme" Steven Withrow and me has been a truly satisfying project. Though we each offer a sampling of twenty of our own poems, this little tome features two sonnet sequences that are collaborative works. I have to give credit to Steve and his remarkable and extremely innovative imagination for the "seed" concepts for both of these joint efforts.

Each of these two collaborations—"The Exorcised Lyric" and "Toward Solstice Station"—presented challenges to our shared love of and practice of traditional metered and rhymed verse. Both of these sequences were, essentially but not strictly, done in alternation between us—although in each sequence there is a bit of variance from a "tennis match" back-and-forth or a sonnet approximation of the Japanese "renga" linking (done collaboratively between two or among multiple poets, alternating between haiku sections [which we approximate in English with a three line poem of 5-7-5 syllables] and shorter sections of 7-7 count). The similarity to the much-different Japanese tradition and practice is in the "springboarding" of one poet off the preceding work on the sequence—especially the immediately preceding section, in this case: sonnet.

As per our agreements on these two sequences, the theme and overall concept were clearly understood, but freedom existed as to the individual inspirations and composition of our own sections. With "The Exorcised Lyric" there was also freedom to explore various forms of the sonnet's required 14 lines, but keeping the interlocking requirement of the "Crown" [in this case "Double Crown" (14 poems rather than 7)] The last line of each sonnet must be repeated (or nearly so, with some allowable shifts of exact phrasing) as the first line of the next.

But our work on "Toward Solstice Station" was much more form-restricted, in that we agreed to use Alexander Pushkin's invented sonnet form, usually called, simply, the "Pushkin Sonnet," but also known as the "Onegin Stanza," since it was the form developed and used by that great author in his novel done entirely in sonnets, *EUGENE ONEGIN* [Евгений Онегин]. This form has a very precise rhyme and metrical pattern and makes use of both masculine [accent on the ultimate syllable] and feminine [accent on the penultimate syllable] required rhyming. The scheme is iambic tetrameter as follows, with the lowercase letters indicating a line requiring feminine rhyme—done by adding an extra unaccented syllable at the end of the line: aBaBccDDeFFeGG.

This is far easier to do in Russian than in English due to the ending inflections for case or part of speech in the former tongue that our language has, essentially, dropped—modern English getting its meanings chiefly from word order (syntactical position) rather than from the endings formerly seen in Anglo-Saxon.

Steven Withrow and I have a symbiotic relationship as poets. Hardly a week passes when we're not "bouncing" roughs or finished poems off one another for criticism and comment. In that way, we've—to put it one way—"cross-inspired" one another. And some of the eventual poems that have "transpired" in each of our poetic bodies of work have been helped along by our small mutual admiration ("mutual inspiration") society.

Both of our collaborative sequences should, I hope, help to convince the reader that the mantra chanted by many *vers libre* poets of "Content Dictates Form" is clearly fallacious. Driven by shared themes and concepts, Withrow and I had our forms to be filled with content: more "loosely" the sonnet as quatorzain with "The Exorcised Lyric," but much more "tightly" the Pushkin Sonnet with "Toward Solstice Station." The point is, by analogy, to quote from one of my poems: "...liquid fills the shape it's poured into." So too in poetic creation. Form and Content, Content and Form. Either can precede and inspire the other.

I must also give both credit and appreciation to Mutartis Boswell for the amazing cover design and illustrations that greatly enrich this tome of our shared and individual verses. He wonderfully translated our poetic visions into splendid graphic realization (or "*unreal*-ization" as the case may be).

I hope the reader finds enjoyment and satisfying entertainment in the poetry, both our collaborative efforts and our twenty-each, select individual poems; and images, both verbal and pictorial, herein presented.

Poet's Preface
by Steven Withrow

When I'm writing a story in verse—a mode of language in which something, usually the number of syllables, is counted line by line—I'm asking myself all the questions a prose storyteller asks. For example:

Am I boring or confusing the reader?

Does the structure I'm building stand up?

Does my ending feel unexpectedly inevitable?

I might also ask myself, "Why does this story need to be told in verse?" The need is the crux, and often I will answer, "It doesn't." Proceeding in prose, then, is almost always the better choice, since prose is the norm.

And, as I see it, writing in verse leads to an additional question:

What if the reader doesn't know how to read a poem?

Part of the reader's knowledge is about learning specific technical information (i.e., the basics of prosody), but the larger part is about honing good instincts: how long to pause at the end of a line; how to use the meter to navigate and clarify a dense passage of syllables; how to register the variations in the metrical pattern, with natural intonation, to avoid a monotonous reading.

It is reasonable to expect the reader to arrive at one's prose story having read dozens or hundreds of other prose stories in various styles and genres. There is ample preparation and a degree of familiarity there.

A similar expectation is not as reasonable in poetry. Even among poets and poetry editors, the number of poems read—and read well—can be scarily low. Skimmers of poems are everywhere; readers, not so much.

I am grateful to Frank Coffman and Paul "Mutartis" Boswell for creating this book with me. They are both exceptional artists and, more importantly, they are also excellent readers.

Thank you for being here!

TABLE OF CONTENTS

"...I think our Great Adversary
Is plaguing your person and your pious verses.
A minion Demon dark makes your lines vary,
Guiding your hand, possessed by dreadful curses."

THE EXORCISED LYRIC, 1901
A DOUBLE CROWN OF SONNETS
BY FRANK COFFMAN AND STEVEN WITHROW

I

The poem was haunted. Infernal fiends held sway
Over its prosody and perfect rhymes.
Its author was the preacher Barron Grimes,
Whose journal of the twenty-sixth of May,
The year McKinley died, contains this play
On words: "As Poe had his bells, so I've my chimes.
I've shunned vers libre and all Parisian crimes,
Yet look—my measure's now in disarray,
My careful couplet endings misaligned."
A single reading of the poet's quotes,
Devoid of context for his odd remarks,
Might merely show how Reverend Grimes designed
His lines, but scholars acquainted with his notes
Hear something queer in "An Ascension of Larks."

II

A queer undertone in "An Ascension of Larks"
Sounds through "between the lines," as some discern.
This noted variance—along with Grimes' remarks,
His journal jottings—made me want to learn
More details about the shaping of this poem.
And what I've found either shows a mind diseased
Or reveals events that lead my mind to roam
Past reason!—to conclude that poem was seized
By forces inexplicable, beyond the realm
Of rationality. Yet I must conclude
The poem was plagued by forces that overwhelm
All natural law. And sometimes they intrude
Into our zone—they freely come and go
In this "reality" we think we know.

III

In this reality we think we know,
There are adepts of art and lesser lights
Who prove the masters masterful. By rights
My subject, Grimes, would surely fall below
Only the greatest talents reaching heights
Of vision and technique to rival Poe—
Though that assessment's controversial, so
I'll link the reverend with the Gothamites,
A ragged group of New York writers who
Had vanished much too soon from academe
And who never had a faddish readership.
Although "Larks" failed to make much of a blip,
While arguably deserving high esteem,
Grimes wouldn't live to see 1902.

IV

Grimes wouldn't live to see 1902.
That fact alone adds to the mystery
Surrounding this rare poem. But what is true—
Based on his journaling of its history—
Is his claim the lines he'd penned would weirdly change.
"I saw the rhyme I'd made the night before
Was altered on the page! Something most strange
Was happening. No, I could not ignore,
At first, but subtle differences, yet I
Saw the graceful line I'd deftly planned...
'To soar toward Heaven's heights'...corrupted! And
Rough syllables were added to the line!
It read: 'Why toward Heaven's lies seek to fly,
When you realize descent is the Great Design?'"

V

When you realize descent is the great design,
When it's obvious the tidal pull has turned,
You don't think, "Ah, that epiphany is fine."
More likely, you will question all you've learned
And will flail about until you've settled down
To memorize the new rules of the game.
For Barron Grimes, born in Cooperstown
Decades before the Baseball Hall of Fame,
The shift in paradigm was more abrupt.
He'd long believed in spirit. Magic, though—
Tricks with no sacred source—was rot. He cupped
His hands over his ears in dissent, or so
It seemed, when charlatans would try to sell
The séance craze. He'd see those frauds in Hell.

VI

"The séance craze! He'd see those frauds in Hell,"
He'd written in his journal. It would be
Almost a quarter-century until
Houdini's book condemned the fakery
Of séances. But fifty-odd years before,
The Fox sisters' false claim of clairvoyance—
Though later confessed as hoax—began the lore
Of spirit communication. "A foul annoyance,
I thought at first. In sermons and in text,
In my poetry and tracts, this sacrilege,
Defying Holy Law, had only vexed—
But how to explain this strange and altered page?
I'm sure of the wording of my crafted line.
It must have been changed by human hand—not mine."

VII

"It must have been changed by human hand—not mine."
But must it have? As a skeptic, I'd need proof,
Or at least some sensible evidence, to believe
In a spectral cause. And yet I can conceive
(If my colleagues pressed me, I'd remain aloof)
Of creatures out of *It* or *Frankenstein*.
(That's telling more of me and less of Grimes.)
Was Grimes deluded, then? There is his brother,
Thomas—I've written of his stays at Hearst;
How the poet wrote him, even when the worst
Of Tom's "black moods" would scare their doting mother.
Did illness mangle meter and twist rhymes?
In the entry that follows, two days on, we find
A startling phrase that shows his state of mind.

VIII

The startling phrase that shows his state of mind
Proves just how suddenly a mind can change
If confronted by facts—no matter how bizarre.
Grimes writes of being more and more resigned
To the truth of forces supernatural, strange
Beyond the realm of reason. Things that unbar
And fling full wide whatever door exists
Between this world we think we understand
And somewhere else! "Another altered verse!
How can it be? But, though my mind resists,
I can't explain revisions—in MY hand!—
No memory of these changes. It's a curse!
Before my eyes, it seems that I have penned:
'From Depths of Darkness once more I ascend!'"

IX

"From depths of darkness once more I ascended."
Not I, but I'd be lying if I pretended
I haven't felt a similar sense of lift
From blank despair. Enough of me. Let's shift
Our focus now to how Grimes finally ended
The peculiar rearrangements that emended
(Or so he wrote) his unsung masterpiece.
He tells us that the edits did not cease,
And as a man of the cloth—a Calvinist
At heart, by sect a Universalist—
He looked for hallowed methods of release,
Convinced that only God could grant him peace:
"Demonic presences confuse my eyes;
I give my sins to Him to exorcise."

X

"I give my sins to Him to exorcise,"
Grimes wrote. And then began a week-long session
Of penitence and prayer, sincere confession,
Each minor lapse recalled, the whitest lies
His memory could bring to consciousness
Were chronicled in a litany of contrition—
All meant to lift his verses from perdition.
Yet all was futile! Hopeless! Cursed! Unless?...
"Of course!" he wrote. "As subject of this blight
I tried to 'lift myself by my own bootstraps'—
As they say. I need external aid! Perhaps?..."
And so the caller at the door next night
Was one whom Grimes most gladly welcomed in.
Friend, priest, and exorcist was Michael Quinn.

XI

Friend, priest, and exorcist was Michael Quinn.
(It was Tom, in fact, who introduced the men,
The year he left his teaching post at Penn,
Joined the Catholic Church, and quit the gin.)
Taller than Lincoln, with a jutting chin,
The Irishman stood, austere, in the den,
His silhouette fixed like a fine-tipped pen,
His scarecrow frame insupportably thin.
Grimes almost balked at bringing Quinn inside
What he'd come to think of as his "secret room"
(In an earlier journal entry: "sanctum space")
And wished he'd burnt his papers, petrified
That Father Quinn would read in him a doom
No Christian expiation could erase.

XII

"No Christian expiation can erase
Our Enemy's vast Evil, but we can,
Through God's great might and prayer, return to Grace
And Hope—restore the Light—in any man
Not irredeemable. And very few
Sink to that depth. And you, my troubled friend,
Are nowise numbered in that curséd lot,"
Said Quinn. Yet, seeing the altered lines, he knew
Much work was needed now to bring an end
To the poet's plight, rub out each evil blot
On his rhymes. "I think our Great Adversary
Is plaguing your person and your pious verses.
A minion Demon dark makes your lines vary,
Guiding your hand, possessed by dreadful curses."

XIII

"Guiding your hand, possessed by dreadful curses."
Three hours of words and gestures to expel
An ink-encrusted incubus from Hell
Depleted Grimes of faith...He conjured nurses
Tending to Tom at Hearst, the acid smell
Of disinfectant, the heavy plod of hearses
Down horse-muck streets, a murder of crows disperses
As they pass, their parents dead, a funeral bell
Clanging, clanging...His jottings say that Quinn,
On finishing his rites, could see he'd failed
His friend and quickly fled the room in silence.
That's where his journal ends. Neat as a pin?
Unfair? It kills me not to know what ailed
The poet, and why he took his life in violence.

XIV

Yes, Barron Grimes, he took his life in violence—
He cut his wrists in a tub; his landlord found him
Floating in, the papers said, "dead silence"—
And to this day conspiracies surround him.
I wrote my master's thesis to debunk
The silliest of these. A gay romance
With Quinn, a gambling debt, a girl...such junk!
They treat his suicide as happenstance
Or the last link in a causal chain, no more.
I'm hardly Hercule Poirot or Sherlock Holmes,
But I'm still convinced that Grimes unlocked a door
That will not close, through "Larks" of all his poems,
And I'll risk my hard-won tenure here to say:
That poem is haunted. Infernal fiends hold sway.

An Ascension of Larks
By Rev. Barron Grimes
(His last poem. Called by some the "Suicide Note Poem")

What? Yet again this cacophony, this bird-born song of the lark?
Sure as the morning comes, nay! more sure, quite soon will rise the Dark.
This lark, these larks, in seeming free flight do but taunt
My spirit. How can their flight lift when Hell-thoughts haunt,
When this world of woes, tear-vale, prevails upon my soul?
When my old faith is in fragments—long since it has been whole.
Why smile when this morning wind holds demons of the air?
Pazuzu's minions, frightful fiends! I can almost discern them there
In this morning sky tint, the same pale-blue pallor of the recent dead.
Soon I shall join them; any release is preferable instead
Of these thoughts, these doubts, this torrent of torments that burns
Into my brain! At least, as yet, that mind still lives and sorely learns:
Though these larks may ascend the sky, my soul must soon descend.
I set aside my will and quill and—most welcome now—The End.

An Ascension of Larks
By Rev. Barron Grimes
(Reconstructed by scholars from assorted journal notes, 1901)

...then my state,
(Like to the lark at break of day arising
From sullen earth) sings hymns at heaven's gate;
—Shakespeare, Sonnet 29

Thou melodious time-honoured symbol of the morn,
Whose bright song, like sunlight, seems from all beauties born.
Praise be to Thee, who hast uplifted me
From sullen melancholy to fly, sky—brave and free.
Thou and thy brothers sail the winds, the very air
That's Life to all—the ocean that thou dost fare—
Well hath taught my troubled spirit to soar
And hath renewed my shaken Faith once more.
Yea! That recent time of Hardship's pains, Doubts dark
Hath been quite lifted from my soul, Friend Lark!
For if Creation shows such wondrous powers,
Whether in wind-whipped night rain or in bright morning hours,
Why should I doubt my Creator's Hand hath sent
These wonders to bless my soul's, these larks' ascent.

NOTA BENE: REV. BARRON GRIMES AND THE CONTROVERSIES SURROUNDING HIS POEM "AN ASCENSION OF LARKS"
BY DR. HOWARD CHAMBERS ASHTON, BROWN UNIVERSITY

For decades, the accepted version of Reverend Barron Grimes' "An Ascension of Larks"—well-known as his last poem left in manuscript [dated 29 June 1901] before the publication of his final collection and often labeled as his "suicide poem"—was the despairing text that is given above as the official version. But his sensational journal entries from the weeks before and up to the time of his suicide have been studied more closely than the poem itself.

Those entries, recounting Grimes' belief in supernatural, even demonic, interference with his work on this poem, have been considered the products and ramblings of a man deluded, a minister despairing the loss of his faith. Yet, through the work of several scholars in the years since—notably the efforts of Wieland Brown in the next decade, Dame Carmilla Brundage in the 1950s and 1960s, and of Algernon Finlay and myself recently—it seems possible that some credence needs to be lent to the admittedly amazing possibility that something preternatural might indeed have been involved with both the evolution of this final morbid poem and Grimes' self-destruction.

The second "version" of the poem as presented above is, admittedly, only conjectural. Yet through the painstaking piecing together of many disparate journal entries, scribblings on recovered bits of paper, backs of envelopes, and a piece of cardboard in one case—it is now reasonable to conclude that the far more typically themed second poem is at least close to what Grimes intended. This work was facilitated to some degree by the poet's propensity to write in couplets. Several separated verses matched up nicely with regard to meter and sentence sense.

Also, a stylometric analysis program designed to aid in authorship determination, developed through a joint project between the Linguistics and Computer Science departments here at Brown, "completed" lines 3 and 4.

In any case, the two poems offer up quite different worldviews. There is no doubt that the first version is the poem found under his hand and pen upon the discovery of his body. The second poem is offered for the reader's consideration and pondering.

My collection of *The Complete Poems and Journals of the Right Reverend Barron Grimes* was published last year by Gernsbach & Farnsworth, Boston.

II

Twenty Poems by Steven Withrow

The Unruffled Man

I
Gibbons had taken care, in strangling
Warden Kim, to taste the air
Escaping from his lungs. And angling
The body upright in the chair,
Fright-mask frozen, broke his chokehold.
Leaving the room, he thought that so cold
Were the warden's final gasps, they might
Have been enough to make this night
His last and finest strangulation,
But he knew he had to carry on.
He closed the office door. At dawn,
The deputy next on rotation
Would open it and find Kim dead.
He left the prison, went home to bed.

II
When he became a guard, Roy Gibbons
Was one year out of Pakistan,
A jarhead wearing valor ribbons,
A singularly unruffled man.
He didn't need the perps to fear him;
Spoke forcefully so all could hear him
Clear across the yard. But soon
A problem came, one afternoon
While overseeing the mealtime shuffle.
The inmates barely made a noise;
He had to give it to the boys.
It was Henderson who caused a scuffle
And signed his death note, as it were.
Gibbons's thoughts began to blur,

And he couldn't quite recall deciding
To follow the young guard to his truck
At end of shift. No time for hiding,
Gibbons rushed in and, by luck,
Got close enough to grab and throttle.
(The sounds he heard were deep and glottal.)
Henderson went limp and down
As quickly as a man can drown.
The strangler tasted salt, warm butter,
But felt he couldn't trust the sense,
Too chemical and too intense,
Then rolled the corpse into the gutter.
He pictured this a kind of debt
He knew he hadn't settled yet.

III

Three drifters and a highway worker
Preceded killing Warden Kim.
Police were searching for a lurker,
But nobody suspected him.
At least so far. His combat training
Strengthened his vigilance. It was raining
The day Kim's murder hit the news.
It looked like blood was on his shoes
As he cleared security that morning.
Rust and mud, he assured himself.
He stored his lunchbox on a shelf.
An older guard gave Gibbons warning
That homicide was grilling the staff.
Roy shivered, let out a breathless laugh.

A Partial Confession

I'd tell you that I don't believe in ghosts,
But I'd be lying. Now, the truth of it,
So far as these things go, is I'll admit
To reading certain superstitious posts
On sites like Spooks.com and Haunted Hosts
(Mostly I don't fall for such weird shit)
That got me thinking maybe there's a bit
More to the stories than just empty boasts.

How come I rigged a camera up last night?
Some guys who work the loading dock with me,
They said the warehouse has a poltergeist.
Odd noises, lights. I thought at first I might
Catch proof, see something move, get on TV.
But, Father—I've erased it all... Oh Christ...

A Loose Tooth

I

Tonguing the tooth and wiggling it, he flinched.
 It hurt, and had since morning when he ate
 A raisin bagel. Rushed, already late
For his first appointment, he pinched

His cheek twice, hard, and ran to catch his train.
 His 9:15 had canceled, luckily,
 And so he had a rare few moments free
To wonder at the reason for the pain.

Being an orthodontist, Reynolds knew
 That shifting molars, aging gums, could cause
 A loose bicuspid in the strongest of jaws,
And this did nothing to restrict his true

Virility. He was still a man of action.
 He hit the climbing gym three times a week
 And dated younger women. Sure, his peak
Was past him now. He'd slowed. But this infraction

In otherwise immaculate routine—
 Between the tooth and running late for work,
 This day was an anomaly—would lurk
For hours deep in his mind unless the machine

Of his attention could be routed where
 It would be more effective. Out of habit,
 He twitched his nose and froze, a frightened rabbit,
Then grabbed and tugged a lock of graying hair.

II

He hurried through his patient load till noon
   When he left his uptown office for a bite
   At Earl's Cafe. His loose tooth wobbled right
And left. Seated, he tapped it with a spoon

And flinched again. He couldn't pull it out
   Himself, he knew, so he made a mental note
   To call his dentist. He glanced down at his coat
And saw a spot of blood. He began to doubt

How long he could hold off a dental visit.
   He touched the tooth-top with a fingertip
   And pulled back, yelping, as another drip
Of red plashed on his plate. "A bleeder, is it?"

He whispered. Stood up, headed for the can,
   Where a tiny mirror hung above a sink.
   The light was dim enough to make him think,
Gawking at his face, "Now, there's a man

Who'd frighten little kids. I look so white,
   So old, so paper-thin." He leaned in closer.
   His visage there was growing grosser, grosser,
And the loose tooth, top row left, had turned a bright

And gamma-radiated green. He spluttered.
   "What the fucking hell?!" he asked the mirror.
   He rubbed his eyes, but it wasn't any clearer.
"I'll rip you out," the orthodontist muttered.

III

Outside, having left his lunch and paid
 His bill with too much cash, he lurched across
 The street to a shop that sold the dregs and dross
Of living. And like a freak in a masquerade,

His teeth agleam, he staggered down an aisle
 To a rack of tools. He stopped, and there it was:
 A pair of pliers, needle-nosed. A buzz
Of unexpected pleasure made him smile.

He walked out, a smiling fool despite the ache,
 And shouts of thievery did not disturb
 His gait. He couldn't wait. He sat at the curb
And with the pliers seized the wriggling snake.

A wrench, and then a crack, to have it whole.
 A bloody lump of lozenge shape and size.
 He held the thing up nearer to his eyes
And cackled, spitting venom from his soul.

When the cops came, he lost the strength to resist.
 They led him to a squad car, cuffed and calm.
 His tooth extraction was the healing balm
He needed, or so it seemed. A therapist

Is surely in his future, but for now
 He's savoring his simple victory.
 He stumbles at a clicking in his knee.
He'll fix that later, too. No matter how.

Your Sunday Shirt

I leave your laundry swaying
On the line behind the shack,
With our bloodhound outside baying,
But I'm not looking back
At the red splotch on the shoulder
    Of your Sunday shirt;
That stain has started to molder,
      And isn't dirt.

I might have let it burn up
In the wood stove as I did
Your meal of beef and turnip,
And the stray red hairs you hid,
From the slain girl, in the curtain
      Beside our bed,
But I wanted to be certain
      I've hanged what's dead.

And I could have called a neighbor
Or left you to police,
Yet I took on the labor
When you said she was your niece,
And you said it close to proudly,
      And I was your wife,
And you said it again, more loudly—
      So I used a knife.

A Visit with Mrs. Pike

As part of her new job, Yvette drove down
To Ring's Neck, where her boss's wife,
The ailing Mrs. Pike,
Lived now, alone.
It seemed she'd come to like
To manage her husband's working life
As much as when she'd lived with him in town.

(If the law firm didn't pay Yvette so well,
And she hadn't yet been picked to lead
A major corporate case,
She might have thrown
This "meeting" in Pike's pink face—
Did someone with her skill set need
To curtsy for a sagging wife-from-hell?)

Yvette thought Pike's lake house would be immense
With gables and a turret guard,
So it surprised her when
She saw a stone-
Walled bungalow, with Zen
Or Shinto statues in the yard.
She parked on dirt; she took her phone for self-defense.

Old Mrs. Pike, who stood on a walking bridge,
Was younger by ten years at least
Than Yvette had ever guessed.
Her smooth skin shone
With health; she was simply dressed.
As she spoke, her restful forehead creased.
"You like a drink? There's fruit juice in the fridge."

Yvette was so amazed she didn't answer,
And the older woman grinned and said,
"My water garden. Yes,
It's a world of its own.
And I feel I should confess:
My husband painted me half-dead?
It's true I'm sick, but not with any cancer."

Approaching her, Yvette could see a crescent
Of sculpted pond, knee-deep, on tarp,
A languid spring-fed streaming,
A tranquil zone
Of lucid water, teeming
With big brocaded fish. "My carp.
My precious koi. So dear and iridescent,"

The young-old woman said, her voice still cheery.
"Look closer." Yvette did. She bent
At the edge, off-balance, and...
She felt her phone
Vibrating in her hand.
A text from Pike. Two words he sent:
"I'm sorry." What the—?! This, she thought, is eerie.

She dropped her phone. The koi below had changed.
The dozen or so had doubled in size,
Their bubbling water muddy.
Contorted bone
And burnished scales turned bloody.
Piranha teeth and great white eyes.
It made no sense. She had to be deranged.

The koi swam circles, snapping at the air.
A hard shove, and she toppled in.
A splash, a liquid blast.
A stifled groan.
And Mrs. Pike, at last,
Watched severed fingers float. A chin
Bobbed up. Then lips. Then hair. Then nothing there.

And Mrs. Pike, at last,
Watched severed fingers float. A chin
Bobbed up. Then lips. Then hair. Then nothing there.

After Doctors Failed Her

He pushes her wheelchair across the stage,
And the healer comes up: "You believe in the Source?"
He secretly hopes his mother will force
Him to turn her around, flushed with rage.
The trickster reads him. His mother nods
In the vise of the chair, and sees absent gods.

He, having been raised to predict her needs,
Speaks out for his mother, who signs commands:
"We'll follow wherever your power leads.
We're willing." And then the man lays hands
On both their startled heads; he chants—
Words—no, it's in tongues! Binds them in a trance.

He wakes in a pew of an empty church,
Alone. No stage, no man. Are his eyes,
He thinks, in another's face? He tries
To stand, and with a sickening lurch,
Slumps over, numb. In a glass tableau
His mother walks on, saintly and slow.

Great-Uncle Horace

Great-Uncle Horace has the head of a hawk,
  And a beak-shaking shriek is his manner of talk.
His wife, Two-Faced Janice, is not of my blood;
  She's been holding her tongues since the Year of the Flood.

In the outermost twigs of my family elm,
  There are frost giants posing as peers of the realm;
And, if we are a book, still the thrillingest chapter
  Stars Hawk-Headed Horace—that Son of a Raptor!

Incident on Crescent Spit

It was after I first caught sight of the dune
    That I knew I'd never escape the spit.
I'd come as a tourist, to glimpse the unknown,
    As many had then, but the thrill of it
For me was dashed, since I was to learn
That to touch the sand was not to return

To the world beyond the dune. The guide
    Had called it "Poseidon's Pyramid";
It might have been the tomb of a god,
    Looming above the sea as it did,
Though it had no builders but the hands
Of the wind and the tide that shaped the sands.

That stretch of beach stuck out like the moon
    In its waxing phase, and the whole site
Was cordoned off from visitors then.
    The signs proclaimed the island's right
To bar us; the dune was tall enough,
At least, to see from a nearby bluff,

But I had to get closer. I bribed a guard
    (It wasn't my first, or worst, offense)
And slipped at night, unseen, unheard,
    Through a gate below the dune. Immense
It was, and it seemed to pulse with the sound
Of the surf, its grumbling shaking the ground.

When I reached its base, I started to climb—
    Sinking with each step up to my thighs,
The sand was so soft—to add my name
    To those who'd scaled its shifting rise
Before it was off-limits. I stopped
Halfway; the slope beneath me dropped

Into a pit, and I tumbled in,
    Scrabbling and kicking as I fell—
And I'm falling still. The sand is fine
    And black around me in this well
Of slowly eroding souls. If I drown
In the sea, I'll keep on going down.

The Fetch
(fetch: a doppelgänger;
a ghostly counterpart of a living person)

Sentenced to six years straight for armed assault,
My third incarceration and my worst,
I steel myself for go-numb days, and nights
With no sound sleep, when, weeks in, there's my daughter
(Christine's girl, Marnie—must be twenty-one)
Beyond the glass, a visitor; I reach
To take the phone as she holds out a photo.

A man who must be me, but sharper, cleaner—
Am I the evil twin?—is smiling near
A stream, his arm around a laughing Marnie.
Camping, or on a summer hike, they are
A model father-daughter pairing, yet
This absolutely cannot be; we never...
But no, I am not present in this picture.

How? I mouth, immobile. Mimicking,
She slowly answers: All my life. No dad.
I wished. (Her eyes light up.) And I got my wish.
I stare. Again, I go to take the phone,
But she stands and walks, contented, from the room,
Leaving the photo. Their faces hold me down;
It takes two guards to haul me to my cell.

Glenwell's Son

In Albert's mind, the uninvited one
At each work fête was Glenwell's murdered son.
The dead boy came to office feasts—he haunted
The August sales retreat, a thing unwanted—
But Glenwell had his name above the door,
So younger staffers gasped and said no more.

The year the dead boy's body met the worm
Was the first of Albert's tenure with the firm.
A drifter had surrendered and confessed;
Still, Glenwell's son seemed disinclined to rest.
Now, at the Christmas singalong, each note
Sticks like a thumb in Albert's guilty throat.

The Wrong Stop

I fell asleep while on the bus;
  Forgot to pull the cord.
The driver I named Gloomy Gus
  Pressed onward as I snored.

I woke up with a jolt, and I
  Could tell the time was wrong.
The afternoon had left the sky—
  The lunar light was strong.

Across, another rider, tall
  And skeletally thin,
Was whistling with a dying fall,
  But I cannot begin

To say—I'd lost all sense of place—
  Where I had seen his kind
Or how his wasted wax-doll face
  Had meddled with my mind.

His piping paused; he didn't speak,
  So I could hear a bell
Colliding with the engine's shriek
  As Gus called, "Next stop—Hell."

I turned. My window showed a field
  Of devastated grain;
Its locust-ridden rows appealed
  To the sick parts of my brain.

Then a borderland where biting flies
  The size of great horned owls
Patrolled the close, necrotic skies.
  That's when I caught the howls

From cauldrons boiling naked damned
   That followed on our tour.
I shot up, reached the back, and slammed,
   In panic, on the door.

"I'm dreaming! No! It's just a dream!"
   I hollered myself hoarse.
I crumpled, wept. I couldn't scream,
   So Gus obliged, of course.

"I'm dreaming! No! It's just a dream!"

Hissing Bird

When Myron Dunn described the hissing bird
He'd spotted on a potentilla shrub,
It stupefied the Portland Birding Club,
Of which, at ninety, he was but the third
Most senior member. "I wouldn't trust my word
Were I in your position. 'Prove it, bub,'
I'd say. So I advanced to solve that rub
By making us a tape. And once you've heard
The tomcat noise the little thing gives out,
You'll want to see it for yourselves." Dunn stood
And played the tape, and there, beyond a doubt,
A spitting shrill that was unlike the rasp
Of any bird in eastern Maine. It could,
Eve Perkins said, be Cleopatra's asp.

That afternoon, Dunn saw the bird again
And this time had his camera set to snap
The almost-chickadee, with tawny cap
Instead of black and wings like a small red hen.
The bird was at his feeder, silent when
He first approached, but now began to flap
And hiss as though, in close, he'd sprung a trap
That sounded an alarm. He shuddered, then,
Because its viper voice had multiplied.
From neighbors' gardens several blocks away
Came cirrus clouds of rasping red-capped clones
That battered at his body, cracking bones.
His line of mourners, later, could not say
How Myron Dunn, his casket closed, had died.

Caged Animals
(After Robert Frost's "Ghost House")

The girl I was was a timid mouse
When we came to stay at the summer house
  Of Crazy Jane, my mother's friend.
  (She earned that nickname, in the end.)
She had no children, nor a spouse;

She seemed to be from a grander age
Of passenger ships, or the opera stage;
  Wore dressing gowns and her hair pinned up;
  She served me tea in a china cup;
And she kept a cockatoo in a cage.

The white-bodied bird had a yellow crest,
A curved black bill. And as a guest,
  Though shy of Jane, I could approach
  That imposing cage and quietly coach
Him to mimic a phrase: You love me best.

I fed him grapes as we worked on words;
He wasn't among the most brilliant birds,
  But we practiced for hours. Then Jane swept in
  While Mom was resting: "You won't be kin
To creatures till you've joined their herds

Or flocks; have dwelt in the fox's den
Or the honeybee's box." And when
  I tried to ask her how she knew
  So much about the cockatoo,
She signed the air, in feather pen,

And thus transformed me. Here I perch,
The white bird's mate. I've ceased my search
  For methods of escape. She turned
  Mom to a toad, and I have learned
To be stone, like a gargoyle on a church.

Jane visits us less frequently,
But she adds to her menagerie
  Each time she does. There's now a crow
  Who used to be a man, and a doe
With a woman's eyes. And I can see

My mate was once a human boy.
We cannot speak, but still enjoy
  The silences. (Mom died last year.)
  Strangely, there's an egg, I fear,
To save from Jane, I must destroy.

...Crazy Jane, my mother's friend.
(She earned that nickname, in the end.)

The Burning Man

The burning man is after me;
He ate the forest, tree by tree.
He's slim of limb and thin of skin.
He rings the flaming orchard in
His arms of Agent Orange, and
A swarm of aphids in his hand.

The burning man has eaten well,
And by his leavings I can tell
He favors cherry over pear;
He flings the pits, a browsing bear;
But even though he's sated, he
Will clear another plate for me.

The burning man is instant blight:
An ash-black thumb, a torch to light
The stubble fields in Stygian mist
Like kindling for an arsonist.
I can't deter him, nor assuage;
He hunts for pleasure, not for rage.

The burning man is growing wise
To where I run. His mantis eyes
Are now protruding to the sea—
Too soon he will be done with me—
Up the headland, down the pier:
His wicker crown is here, is here!

A Means of Summoning
For M.R. James

Wry spirit, sessile as a pondweed, wake.
Sleep does not become you, nor the ebb
Of water through a water spider's web,
So large the diving bell could catch a snake
Where striders cross the wobble of the lake
To end life in a mallard's yellow nib,
The opposite of Eve from Adam's rib,
For any sense these correlations make.

In "A Warning to the Curious" you'll note
One squat martello tower on a bluff
(As troublous now as was it when you wrote)
Is, in its way, analogous enough
To how your soul has settled to rebuff
The notion that Old Scratch should hold your coat.

Fumbling the Transfer

At the border station
   Sheltered from the rain
Soldiers on the platform
   Await the train

Hauling the monsters.
   Air brakes shriek.
The driver signals
   But doesn't speak.

Cages uncoupled,
   The engine goes
To the army train yard
   And never slows.

Back at the border
   The grunts are lax
In shunting the boxcars
   To other tracks.

A cage cracks open;
   A Sharp One runs.
The soldiers closest
   Drop their guns

As hands are severed,
   Heads get lopped—
Cursing the late train
   Ever stopped.

We Cannot Keep That Cat

We cannot keep that cat,
And nobody will make us.
I'll bathe in bleach before
I let it overtake us.
We cannot keep that cat.

I did not ask for this.
You found it in the alley.
We'll send that fiend to die
Of sunstroke in Death Valley.
I did not ask for this.

We cannot keep that cat.
I swear it thinks we're dinner.
And can't you see it's grown
Much taller now, but thinner?
We cannot keep that cat.

Goblin's Nest

A windfall branch brought down the goblin's nest.
My brother, playing out after the storm,
Discovered it among the line of oaks
That marked our acre from the woods beyond.
With him just eight and me thirteen, our bond
Was close, which helped in weathering the jokes
Of neighbor boys whose brains could not perform
The calculations needed to contest
Their notion that a gulf of five years ought
To be unbridgeable. Shouting for me
To come and look, the day the goblins fell,
He pulled me from my reading, and to tell
It now, I'd like to say that I could see
The nest for what it was, but I could not.

I saw a blue jay's nest: a sturdy cup
Of roots and twigs entwined with strips of bark.
My eyes said empty; eggs or hatchlings, none.
My brother saw at once—and here my age
Betrayed me—seven goblins in a cage.
He spoke. I saw them too. We worked as one
To hide the nest in leaves as it grew dark,
Then went inside. Entranced, we both stayed up
(We still had shared a room that year) till dawn.
We failed to puzzle out what we had found
Or how to end the spell. We quickly dressed,
Snuck downstairs, through the door, and to the nest.
Clearing the leaves, we bit our tongues. The ground
Beneath was wilting grass. Our bridge was gone.

Housewife's Lament, Wartime

The numinous, if it exists,
Must be in the mending
And making lists.

In the thwack of a dishrag
That thins an infant's sleep.
(Husbands are oblivious.)

In the amnion
Of blackout curtains
Hide angel embryos...

What useless rhapsody!
I ace the crossword;
Clip obits from the Times.

From photo albums
A maudlin découpage
Of weddings, outings,

Trims my dressing table.
A line of tiny ants
Is coming from the wall—

It's spring already—
By crippling them
I hobble the asomatous

(Wry, expensive word)
And half-expect the baby
To wake with whooping cough;

Such are my fears.
The numinous, if I've a say,
Is weekly rations, daily tears.

The Cruel Become Werewolves

The cruel contract lycanthropy and grow
More visibly hirsute. The moon is not
Involved, unless a charge of lunacy
Is warranted, and some say this is so,
But no one's offered evidential proof,
And God knows if it's cursed or if it's caught.

To illustrate the change, we'll cite the case
Of Morris Incaviglia, salesman for
Amalgamated Sundries Limited,
Who drove a yellow Saab from place to place
And would seek out, when circumstance allowed,
A pass-through town without a country store

For many miles, and then he'd settle on
That town's most precious landmark; it could be
A covered bridge now closed to cars, a church
The founders built, its first bell tower gone
In some great winter storm, but still a gem,
Or even just an ivy-tangled tree

At the town's lone four-way stop. And finding it,
The salesman would return at night to toss
A Mason jar of flaming kerosene
Straight at its most incendiary bit.
He'd often lob a second or a third,
Ensuring it would be a total loss.

Then Morris, groomed impeccably, would drive
Until the razored stubble on his cheeks
Became a scraggly beard. His canine teeth
Would lengthen, too. But he felt no more alive,
And with less wolfish strength, than when he burned.
We estimate he'd had the plague for weeks.

III

Twenty Poems by Frank Coffman

The Line

Somewhere there's a line, if penned all would be beguiled!
It would chill all hearts and all souls terrify.
Dark poets have sought it in the deeps of sky,
In winds that whip the willow rushes wild,
In black pools, where the waters never lie
Quite restless, in stark images beviled,
In words of horror upon horror piled!

But rare and few those poets who came nigh
To crafting such a line with weirding art:
Poe sought to find that powerful verse accursed.
And Lovecraft strove such horror to impart,
And many since believed it could be versed.

Perhaps it's best that line should never be.
Who knows what—through its chant—might be set free?

He Who Waits

I am the Watcher, and I stand in wait.
As long as Life has lasted on this Earth:
The hells of human tragedy, the heights of mirth,
The deeper happinesses, and the depths of hate.
All, all I've seen: the ends of Chance and Fate,
The years that bounty and the years that dearth
Have spun around this old Orb since its birth,
I've watched and waited here beside *The Gate*.

Oh yes, I have been waiting all these years,
Was ancient when Atlantis met its doom,
Watched Babel's Tower and great Pyramids grow.
I know the range of mankind's hopes and fears.
And know the thing most fear most is the tomb.
I wait. *Et in Arcadia Ego.*

Xenomnesia

For untold ages, we have gazed up at the sky,
Amazed at the black, bejeweled, and wondrous welkin wide.
And some have sensed—most strange!—a *soundless voice* on high,
Not speaking words–but thoughts!–that would not be denied:
  "You think you are alone in all this cosmos vast,
  Believe that, in this universe, you are unique?
  Know you that such ideas—foolish!—cannot last.
  Know that you have, at heart, the answer that you seek:
  All, all are gathered from far-flung primordial dust!
  All worlds congeal from multiverses widely thrown,
  And multitudes of other beings—this you must
  Have already surmised—nay! secretly have known."
Such is the Deep Truth of our Alien Memory:
Those stars share both out Past and Distant Destiny.

The Valdemar Effect

He'd been intrigued by one grim tale by Poe
About a mesmerist and the physical effect—
If one sought the craft of hypnotism to know
And put those skills to use—one could direct
A subject so enthralled to imitate
Symptoms of dread diseases—even Death!

But when he realized it was too late—
The pallor and chill of flesh—yes! but the breath
Had ceased now fully fifteen minutes since,
And ten attempts to end the spell had failed—
He fled that abandoned house and hurried thence,
Back to his flat—dreading what he'd unveiled.

They found him one month later in his bed,
Strangled by hands that dropped flesh one month dead.

The Chickcharney Haunts the Wild

The Blue Holes of Andros:
Two Bahamian Legends

On and around Andros trifurcated[1] isle
The Blue Holes beckon divers who would dare
To search their depths. But all such should beware
What lies within those sea-linked ink-dark caves.
The natives know the Lusca [2] dwells down there
And know, for those who meet it, nothing saves
Their reckless life. The great-toothed jaws,
The tentacles—against all Nature's laws!—
That giant horror means Death!
                            Meanwhile
The owl-like, weird Chickcharney[3] haunts the wild,
Surrounding groves and thickets. Those beguiled
Who treat the creature well will be long-blessed,
But those who dare to laugh or to mistreat
That red-eyed, three-toed thing will suffer long,
Their life by constant ills and woes distressed,
Their lot to know a living Hell complete.

Mere Caribbean legends, a folk plainsong?
No! Two beasts plague that weird and wondrous place:
One like a bird of prey with prehensile tail,
A trickster thing that can be bane or boon,
There in the forest pines that hide the moon;
The other a huge cephalopodic shark,
A threat to all who swim, to all who sail
Over blue waters…but the depths are dark.
A Thing of the hidden horrors of "Inner Space."

Notes on "The Blue Holes of Andros"

[1] The Bahamian "Island" of Andros is actually an archipelago, consisting of hundreds of small islets and cays connected by mangrove estuaries and tidal swamplands, it is comprised of three major islands: North Andros, Mangrove Cay, and South Andros. These three main islands are separated by "bights," estuaries that trifurcate the island, connecting the island's east and west coasts.

[2] The Lusca is a creature of Caribbean folklore, known throughout the many islands that are contained within the Bermuda Triangle. Bahamian folklore connects it most directly with the "Blue Holes" (roughly 175 on the island and 25 offshore) that connect to a sub-marine, sub-terrestrial system of caves, most of which have never been explored. Most accounts say that it is a hybrid monster with the head of a shark, but with a tentacled body like an octopus or squid. It is said to be as large as 75 to 200 feet in length.

[3] The Chickcharney is reputed to be an owl-like creature with a prehensile tail, red eyes (or one red eye) and three toes on each foot. This mischievous trickster lives in the thick pine forest and mangrove thickets of Andros and can bestow either blessings or curses upon those who encounter it, depending on how it is treated..

Year's End

Trees skeletal and bare
Stand up like lacework 'gainst the setting sun.
Again begun—
The numbing brushstrokes of the cold night air.

Fiery autumnal leaves
Are covered o'er with hoar. The snow descends.
The old year ends.
And once again the unkept promise grieves.

The best-laid plans were made
By most who swore 'twould be a better year.
But withered, sere
Dead leaves, they lie undone on Hope's sad bier.

A wan moon swiftly sails
Through racing clouds, the welkin's bright points peek
From gaps that streak.
Against wolf-biting wind, the thick cloak fails.

A cheerless sunrise breaks
Over the hills, and all birdsong has ceased.
A fearsome Beast,
Months dormant and at bay, now grimly wakes.

Yet Time will Tick and Tock,
The world will quicken, spring to life once more—
Just as before
Will long years of potential roll and rock.

Beyond The Veil

Some few have journeyed out beyond *The Veil*.
Of those that venture, fewer still come back.
Dark tomes hold hidden spells to look, but lack
The black, archaic words that will not fail
To bring the seeker home to this our realm.
From this side, only shadowy shapes uncertain
Beckon and stir behind that tenebrous curtain,
And what waits there would quickly overwhelm.

Best not to look—but much worse that way to travel,
For its secrets are kept from no living soul forever;
There is time enough to wait for the Hand of Fate.
And those who return are changed. Their minds unravel;
Their rantings hold one theme: a wish they had never
Traversed a path so cursed...but now—too late!

Agon

This is a duel to simplify the thing.
 Instead of thousands, one will battle one,
 And maybe this long struggle will be done.
I'll run no more! I stand for kith and king!

There on the barren plain his foeman stood,
 A warrior of whom 'twas said could not be killed,
 Invincible, in every warcraft skilled,
Who'd left behind a very sea of blood,

Bedecked in golden helm with horsehair crest,
 Cuirass and greaves of bold bronze burnished bright,
 And visage proof he eagered for the fight,
This man aloof—so different from the rest.

Whate'er the Fates have spun, I have no fear.

Smiling defiance—Hector threw his spear.

Ouroboros

I

A symbol older than Egypt's eldritch land,
Where empty, towering tombs in ruin stand,
A Serpent circles, eating its own tail—
Has done so as the nations rise and fail,
Has done thus from the first. Eternity
Of how it was, how it is, how it shall be.
Greeks and Romans, Gnostics and Norse all knew
The "Tail Devourer" shows what's e'er been True:
The Cycles spin—no "widening gyre" to see.
The Circle always gains the victory.
Neither the wide nor narrow can prevail,
No matter how we strive to stop, assail
The spin. The Alternation: that's what's planned.
Those who accept this finally understand.

II

This larger vision of the snake is firm:
The ceaseless cycles of the Circled Wyrm.
Great Jörmungandr wraps around us all;
Of that "enormous magic" we're in thrall.

    Yet, we who dwell within this "Mid-Earth's" coil—
Though living through small cycles, strife and toil,
Through pains, yet pleasures too, both joys and tears,
Pass through our time in a straight line of years!
    The Greater Circles need not flaw nor foil
Our paths from birth to death, need not despoil
Each chance to answer to a Greater Call,
Do deeds worthy of Song—to Rise before we Fall.
Though now within this Dragon wild and wide...
    At last to go beyond and see Outside.

Submission: Never Total
(A Credo)

We send our children out into the wind—
Or, rather, *aether* in this day and age—
To see what fame or fortune they might find
With those who value Words on printed page.
That "printing" too is oft ethereal,
Binary codes that form screen letter shapes,
But, sometimes, ink upon material
Paper that clings, so no great word escapes.
We pray some distant mind will take them in—
But, if they're sadly sent back all unloved,
We confidently send them out again.
Someone will see their virtues and be moved.
We don't prostrate ourselves with piteous plea,
Or bend, grab Zeus's beard, or clasp his knee.

Micro-Organisms

Would we be hideous to them—
Horror show monstrosities—
If they had minds that could hold Terror
Or that brave sense that sees?

Some even serve us in strange ways;
Some kill us with dread disease.
But there's no concept of Right or Wrong
In their DNA's strange keys.

They've no Mind to hold an Evil thought
Or plan a heinous deed;
Of course, no Soul to save or loose,
No Consciousness, Pride, or Greed;
No plan to deceive, nor a heart to break—
Unlike our Macro seed.

Lycan

He who survives the werewolf's baleful bite
Is transformed on the next month's full moon night.
There is no remedy for this vile curse—
Or the Thing he must become!
And neither man nor wolf—but something worse
Will plague the countryside.

He who has seen the wound fade fast, turn white,
And seen *the pentagram* (as it is hight)
Appear there in its place—that man will change!
No hope! He must succumb
On full moon nights—a monster: heinous, strange,
All Nature's laws defied!

He who transforms into this wicked wight
Will often not remember in daylight
What he has done 'neath Luna's glowing face.
There may be only some
Dim memory, if chancing upon the place
Where his own victim died.

He seeks some way to end his horrid plight,
But, finding none, he knows when the moon is bright
And at the full, he'll wend out craving flesh.
There's no escaping from
That change where beast and man will mesh!
As he stalks far and wide.

On full moon nights—a monster: heinous, strange,
All Nature's laws defied!

Words on Ghastly Vellum Writ

"... Perturbe´d men that tremble at a sound,
And ponder words on ghastly vellum writ,
In vipers' blood, to whispers from the night—
Infernal rubrics, sung to Satan's might..."
—George Sterling, from "A Wine of Wizardry"

1.
Mostly unknown, there are some secret tomes
The words of which gloss totalities of Evil.
They hold forbidden chants and cryptic poems
Writ by the hands of those leagued with the Devil.
Some books, beyond the "noonday Devil's" sway,
Contain such horrors from the Depths of Night,
From far beyond our tiny "Milky Way,"
From far beyond the Cosmos' farthest light.

Yet there are those among us who dare to ponder
Those ghastly words on human vellum writ,
Whose souls are doomed to some unholy yonder,
As they to Darkness and Chaos submit.
Beyond all Terrors of our mundane zone,
They beckon Beings who should ne'er be known.

2.
With vile, infernal rubrics these grimoires
Contain foul conjurings and demonic spells
That call up Worldly Evils. But—beyond the stars—
 From a zone of Unimaginable Hells,
"The Old Ones" are summoned with their heinous spawn
To once again engulf our world in Dark.
And Fears more fell than any cloudless dawn
Could hope to cleanse away. Each loathsome mark
Set down in blood of vipers or—of men!—
Has power to motivate fey Nameless Cults
Who seek to summon *Them*, to call *Them* in,
Knowing full well the hideous results,
Seeking with their black-hearted, blasphemous might
To bring the coming of that Endless Night.

Captain Gruchy's Ghost
(A Tale of Old Boston's North End Tunnels)

1.
Old Thomas Gruchy, famous privateer
(elsewise, less politely, known as "pirate")
Picked one cold and gusty day to disappear,
But left—some say—vast treasures that he got
From raids upon French vessels in England's war.
At any rate, there are very few who doubt
There's something beyond the eldritch, brick-sealed door
In the cellar of his queer house on Salem Street.

But why would Gruchy leave Boston town without
His smuggled loot? And some say you could meet—
Somewhere between that arch and Copp's Hill's tombs—
The Captain's ghost! For the tunnel wends that way.
And other darksome legends lower and loom
Above those carved out depths that still hold sway.

2.
Charles Pickman, for one, had a place on Commercial Street,
His cellar held a deep—some say "the Devil's"—well.
It too was covered, sealed so none might greet
Abominations from the depths of Hell.

But Gruchy, so the fables all have told
Amassed an amazing, trove of curséd gold,
And, unglittering in that gloom, are precious jewels.
But those who'd seek such mark themselves as fools.

There sits a small cenotaph atop Copp's Hill,
Marked with the initials T. and G.
Within, well-hidden, a marble trap door still
Awaits the searcher. But best let it be.
For far less would be found—and far more lost!—
In that corridor guarded by Old Tom's ghost.

Rats, corpse-worms, beetles, spiders make a grim wake,
Riding that bone-ribbed vessel—Old Tom their host.
But keeping Horror's hoard safe is Gruchy's Ghost.

3.

For you see, the pirate Captain never left,
Nor did his stores of secret, stolen booty.
Oh yes, he'd planned to keep those fruits of theft,
All of his ill-got, kill-got wealth, the loot he
Had hoarded and stored below that old North street.
But, as he was hefting chests onto the cart,
There were some *Things* in the gloom he chanced to meet—
Things too horrid even for him! They stopped his heart!

So, Thomas Gruchy's bones are still down there,
More rotten than that heart that could not take
The sight of Evils—more than mortal man can bear.
Rats, corpse-worms, beetles, spiders make a grim wake,
Riding that bone-ribbed vessel—Old Tom their host.
But, keeping Horror's hoard safe is Gruchy's Ghost.

Past Tense

"The past never passes.
It simply amasses."
—Brad Leithauser

Though most may think the Present moment's all,
That our lives move through a flowing stream of Now,
We cannot hold tight any tock or tick,
Nor freeze one "frame" of Present. We don't know how.
The Future's seldom clear as moments crawl;
Though Near "To Come's" can often be previewed,
As we seek to peer much farther down that path,
The shapes are lost in haze first, then fog thick
Obscures, then solid wall blocks aftermath.
But, with the Past, there's little to occlude.

There we may travel; through Memory we may stay
And visit Places, Moments, Ghosts of those long gone,
Reverse Time's cycle, trading dusk for dawn.
But—barriers down—*May They also come this way!*

As Summer Turns to Autumn
(A Latvian Daina Sonnet)

Now as Summer turns to Autumn,
On this eve of ancient Samhain,
We are those, the ones who gather,
Practicing the ancient rituals.

See the towering bale-fire blazing;
See the embers flying skyward;
See the Sacrifice we offer;
See the Priest with golden dagger.

Blood we offer up at Midnight.
Drugged and bound upon the altar
Lies the Gift that must be given,
So the land give forth its bounty.

Thus it has been through the ages,
Mother and Green Man, claim these wages.

Negative Space:
Log: 2066.10.31

"My God! all round us now there is a Lack
Beyond the Cosmos' universal black."

I doubt these words will live on to relate
Just what seems now to be our mission's fate.
Our instruments—all working perfectly—assess
That all around our ship...is *Nothingness!*
As if all Time, all Matter were destroyed!
As if this zone is void...of even Void!
And—something—something far beyond all Fear
Makes me feel Something Terrible was here!
Or, rather, Some Ones! But they now have left,
Leaving this zone...of *Everything* bereft!

I can but pray that *They* will never come
To where my crew and I have journeyed from!
This is a negative space that God forgot!
We're never coming back from What is Not!

Dawn of the Night
(A Korean Kasa Sonnet)

Far past the void that we call "Space."
There is a zone of Cosmic Dread
Chaos reigns there. But would rule here;
They—Horrid thought!— seek to return
Where once they dwelt—before expelled:
 Nyarlathotep, Disorder's Lord;
Spawn of Deep Dark, Dread Azathoth;
Grim Yog-Sothoth who guards The Gate
Who IS The Gate, from Nameless Mist
Born long ago.
                        And here on Earth,
Lorn of all hope, we dwell for now,
Do strive to keep our threatened realm.
Dim is that chance, for soon will come
Dawn of that Night!—when Cthulhu wakes.

Halloween/Samain

All Hallow's Eve comes 'round again.
Dusk ushers in the moonlit time,
The darkness that they called Samhain,
The subject of this little rhyme.

The younger folks say, "Trick of Treat,"
Not thinking of the Old Year's Death,
But there are specters you may meet
That chill beyond the frosted breath.

The season that was warm and green
Has now gone by—as seasons must.
And there be things that might be seen
From *Other Zones*, from 'neath the dust.

There is a Darkness that prevails
Far deeper than this cusp of night
Twixt two chill months—And it assails
Our world with monstrous cause for fright.

Know that these children's costumes mock
Those dreaded *Things* that *Do* exist:
Things that have power to more than shock.
Things of grim legends that persist.

This night there is an Open Gate,
Between our "this world" and the next,
That all must pass through soon or late.
But this—of all nights—we are hexed.

Those Horrors that now come this way,
Through this long night of Eldritch Dark—
Though *They* are with us every day—
Tonight are free to wander. Hark!

About us, through this long night's gloom,
Foul fiends of folklore, Terrors of old tales,
Monsters of madness, Ghosts from the tomb—
We think them myths. Yet *They* prevail.

La Villa Infestada:
The Last Pages from
The Journal of Montague LeFanu Blackpool
(A Sequence of Stornello Sonnets)

1.
"Looking back, I still ask, 'How was I to know?'
That villa on the hill had a wondrous view
Of that valley where stretched out the River Po.

It had seemed the perfect place for my retreat—
From this world, yes—but also *Another* that
I'd sought to enter, not knowing what I'd meet!

But I had entered! My God! the horrors met
If one crosses that threshold! And I cannot
Drive them from my mind—though I yearn to forget.

Foolishly, I thought, 'Here…here I will be free
From fell fiends that from that *Nether Zone* did fly.'
I should have known They'd have ways to follow me!

Oh yes, there was a brief span—a few bright weeks….
But a Demon, soon or late, finds what it seeks.

2.
"The days were warm, but shade and evenings cool
September was crawling onward toward the fall.
It seemed my plan had worked. But I was a fool.

On the equinox—a wild and stormy night—
It became clear that the cursed *Forbidden Gate*
I had sought to close again had not shut tight.

The spells I had found in that accursed grimoire
Had worked too well! They had opened wide *The Door*,
And Beings emerged! Some banished long of yore.

I had succeeded by other chants and spells
To send most back to the deepest, blackest Hells.
Soon I learned it doesn't matter where one dwells.

My meddling magic could not be taken back;
Just my living on had left a trail to track!

3.
"So I've fled my hoped for refuge on the hill—
From my villa to the village church. But still
I know *my Nemesis follows*—always will!

I seek unlikely hope of sanctuary,
Here in this holy place, yet I am wary.
I know no balm can heal this Sin I carry.

Father Medici, man of wisdom and grace,
Went up to the villa to exorcise the place.
I cannot forget the look upon his face....

When he returned it was well into the night.
He told me his ministrations had been for naught.
'The Evil in that place is more than cause for fright!

My son, I fear I know not what to do;
I've never met such Powers that now plague you.

4.
"'I will send word to a friend I have in Rome,
The most successful exorcist of our time.
Perhaps he can undo spells from that cursed tome.'
. . .

Today we spent in silence and in prayer
In hopes that the Demon could not enter here.
Thus, we've done all we can think of to prepare.

But now the black night has come. All light has sped.
Looking out, there are no bright stars overhead….
In the chapel…Oh, Dear God! The priest lays dead!

Now I've locked myself into this cellar room,
This dark, dank place befitting the name of 'tomb.'
So ends my tale it seems—a much deserved doom….

It comes!
        Dear Soul, If you read this, understand
Why I chose, at last, a death by my own hand."

IV

TOWARD
SOLSTICE STATION

A SEQUENCE OF PUSHKIN SONNETS

BY FRANK COFFMAN AND STEVEN WITHROW

I
1898

Edith sat up straight and primly
On the padded train-compartment bench.
Beyond the window, shapes moved dimly
As evening rain began to drench
Darkened plains and rural valleys
(In towns, the lamplit lanes and alleys)
That lay beside the railroad track
Like children resting back to back.
She thought of speaking out to mention
A blob that might have been a cow,
But Mother and Father would not now
Give Foolish Edith their attention
(How she could raise such a fuss!)
When they had matters to discuss.

"Oh, Lizzie, you're exasperating!
Even the child knows war with Spain
Is braver than negotiating
A coward's peace. McKinley's reign
Will end, with Cubans left still fighting
Undefended," Father, lighting
His pipe and puffing smoke, remarked.
But Mother, smoothing her dress, was sparked
And almost flamed with indignation.
It took what strength she had to hold
Within her fierce riposte. A cold
Unblinking glare was her oration.
When Father looked away, chagrined,
She crossed herself as though she'd sinned.

Father stood and fled the carriage,
Leaving Mother looking lost
And small. All Edith knew of marriage
Told her it wasn't worth the cost.
(There had to be another option.
Wanting babies? Try adoption.)
Mother reached down for her purse
With the firm hands of a former nurse
And took upon her lap her knitting.
She started on her pillow sham
And whispered, "Damn, damn, damn."
With guilt, she glanced at Edith sitting
Doll-like with her travel dress
And ringlet curls. Said, "What a mess!"

Parents, in Edith's dreams, can't quarrel.
In sleep, she felt her Cleveland house
To be a pleasant home. Immoral
Thoughts and acts were, like a mouse,
Not let inside. They were adoring,
Mum and Dad, less crass and boring
Than they were when she woke. Trips west
Would find them fancifully dressed
As pilgrims or explorers. An only
Child had sisters there, and friends
For parlor games and let's-pretends.
There was no reason to be lonely,
Afternoons, through silent meals...
The train steamed forth on iron wheels.

Later, when Father entered huffing
About "the chilly air tonight,"
Mother stiffened, quickly stuffing
Sham and needles out of sight.
"Please, Arthur, sit," she said, enticing.
He said, "The land around is icing
In freezing rain. It's Illinois
Out there. I asked a porter's boy
How long until we see the city.
He thinks we'll reach Chicago by
The time the dawn sun's in the sky.
Well, that's just how he said it. Pretty
Like that." He coughed, then stamped his feet,
And, removing his hat, resumed his seat.

There was no sleeping car or trundle,
So Edith lay, her body slumped
Against the window on a bundle.
Her parents talked, but she was stumped
To give some terms specific meaning,
Although she listened close, head leaning
Toward the western states. A war
Will spread, and Earth will flood with gore,
Mother murmured.
                    Father answered,
War's a human need. Life takes
From life.
            Mother gasped. That makes
Us monstrous, then—a race of cancered
Soulless hateful husks, she said.
And Edith slept, their words gone dead.

II
1917

The train pulled in to Union Station,
And Edith awakened with a start.
Chicago, "Hub City of the Nation,"
Squealing wheel and creaking part,
A brief cloud of steam—and then a vision
Of bustling folk avoiding collision,
Noises, voices, conductor's call—
It took her a moment to sort it all.
She felt the train car rock in slowing.
Broad, busy platforms far and near!
Only the first "leg" ended here.
This city was not where they were going.
The "Chicago Special" wheezed to a halt.
"It's those damned Huns who are at fault!

"We should be in this war already.
Lusitania was two years ago!"
Her dad's rehearsed speech always steady.
"It doesn't take a genius to know!"
Young Edith was growing very weary
Of this war talk—scary, dreary.
He had the man adjacent's ear—
Who seemed to share her mother's fear:
"But, Sir, it's surely Europe's fracas.
It's not our business. Why shouldn't we
Stay this side of a sheltering sea—
I can't imagine what would make us
Join this affair—take either side,
Protected by an ocean wide."

"Well, there you echo my wife Lizzie
Who claims we're safe: 'Why should we send
Our boys abroad to meet their end?'
You pacifists! All in a tizzy
To shirk the horrors of this war.
History's taught us well before
That sooner's better than too late.
I tell you, Sir, we should not wait!"
At this, she noticed her mother turning
Away from the men and their debate.
Her mother had not smiled of late.
Embarrassed to be mentioned, yearning
To join the talk. But she knew her place,
And hid the flush upon her face.

"Well then, we differ in opinion,
And there's no solving this today.
Although we've neither right nor dominion,
It's likely that you'll have your way;
It certainly seems that we are headed
Down the path your wife and I have dreaded."
So saying, the man looked at his watch.
"I say! I have a train to catch.
I pray you're wrong, Sir." And extended
A hand her father was slow to take,
But, with a nod, gave it a shake.
With that, their conversation ended,
After the man had taken leave,
Mother tugged on Father's sleeve.

"I wish you wouldn't always bluster,"
She whispered. Edith just looked away.
"I swear it takes all the will I can muster
Not to chime in and say my own say.
And when you give my name a mention,
To think I pay you no attention—
It irks me so! And our daughter here
Doesn't need this talk of war and fear,"
Edith looked out the window, ignoring—
At least trying to—her parents' spat.
But then she had an idea that
Might end their squabbling—always boring.
"Father," she asked, "our trip's first 'leg,'
Why is it called that?" She made her eyes beg.

The transfer was made, despite the freezing
Bite of the early April rain.
Mother and Father, set on appeasing
Their talks, as the long Rock Island train
Rumbled westward, on through the gloaming,
Like a serpent in the dimming light roaming
A winding path toward Nebraska.
At a brief stop, there at Omaha
On the platform, as the dull day was dying
On that sixth day of April, they heard
A newsboy calling out a word
That changed the world, for he was crying
A headline no one could ignore—
In banner type, three letters: WAR!

III
1945

Rolling on toward Denver, the train was wending
Past fields of browning corn and wheat.
There'd been little doubt the war was ending;
The Japs would go down to defeat.
A weapon that was most stupendous
(Though Lizzie thought it quite horrendous)
Had been unleashed upon Japan.
A bomb of dreadful power that can
Destroy whole cities in a glowing
Tower of fire. Heat like the sun!
In seconds—centuries undone!
A blast! And then a Death Wind blowing.
And so began a brand-new Age.
Arthur smiled as he turned the page.

The headline shouted Japan's surrender.
"I knew that we would make 'em pay!"
Art beamed, but for Liz it didn't end her
Doubts, didn't lingering fears allay.
The photo showed people laughing, singing
In New York streets. Church bells were ringing
Across the land, both far and near.
But for many it meant a new kind of fear.
With the news of such power new dread was growing:
"Tens of thousands of people killed!"
"Think of all the blood that was spilled!"
Could this power be checked? No way of knowing
Whether the world was cursed or blessed.
Their train and the sun rolled toward the West.

Arthur looked up from the paper remarking,
"Finally! Now just you wait and see—
Our economy's ready. We'll be embarking
To a new era of prosperity."
Liz had to comment. She was dreading
This new age into which they were heading.
"But at what cost? The sacrifice
Of common folk! What a heavy price
In human lives! Did those people merit
Such awful and horrendous death?
To be gone in the span of one short breath?
I fear this world our girl will inherit."
Art replied, "They reaped what they had sown.
There's surely no reason to bemoan

Our enemy's fate. Think of our boys dying
If we'd have tried a land assault!
We'd have lost a million men in trying.
No, no—the enemy was at fault."
Edie sensed there was something greater
Going on. But it didn't make her hate her
Parents quarreling any less.
She understood the world was a mess.
But their "little" war just kept on going.
Through the window, the hills began to grow
Much higher than those she used to know
By the Cuyahoga River flowing
Below their house. She missed that place
On the hill—and the smile on Mother's face.

Arthur was almost twenty years older
Than Liz. A minor "Captain of Industry"
Who'd made his wealth through bold and bolder
Moves in the market. It helped that he
Had inherited the factory. Insulated
Copper wire—thus he was fated,
As a man who made a commodity
Needed "to keep the country free,"
To not have to go off to war and danger.
Liz was intrigued, a bit in awe
Of the handsome man with prospects. She saw
The love of her life. But now, a stranger
Sat by her side in that Pullman car,
A foe to fight in their private war.

There had been years of happy marriage.
Edie was born and all things seemed right.
But two years later, with the miscarriage,
Liz's world became numbed by night.
Edie was too young to miss the brother
She never had. It was the other
Sadness that Mother had most often shown.
It was easy to sense that her parents had grown
Apart. Outside—a new world to discover
"Out West," her mother had said, "we'll have fun."
But so far she hadn't. The train's steady run
Made on through the dark. Her old world was over.
She'd been impressed by the mountainous heights.
Now, up ahead Denver—and millions of lights.

IV
1970

Arthur was more concerned with deadlines
That sunny day in early May,
While Liz was horrified by headlines
On what transpired the previous day.
She found it sickening, horrific—
As the Zephyr rolled on toward the Pacific—
"Arthur, this time they've gone too far.
See how this God-forsaken war
Has gone to killing kids at college!
We both have friends who went to Kent!"
To Liz this marked a new descent.
How could they turn a place of knowledge
Into a terrible killing field?
Back home, in Cleveland, church bells pealed.

"I'll agree they had no reason—
The live ammo was a mistake,
These protests are tantamount to treason,
And something bad was sure to break.
And just how long can we let this go
On?"
      Their destination, "Frisco,"
Was still at least a day ahead.
Edie worked on her sketchpad instead
Of listening to her parents bicker—
One more bout of angry word and frown—
She was drawing a princess in beautiful gown.
The clouds ahead were growing thicker
And blacker—impending thunderous rain.
America, split, was a land in pain.

Two years before, with the Tet Offensive,
At home, as well, battle lines were drawn.
And more and more became apprehensive
Of whether war's darkness would see a dawn.
Then, years beyond the war's beginning,
The question grew: "Can there be any winning
Of this conflict so far from home?"
Stark photos in vivid polychrome,
In newspapers now, but history's pages
Would remember—brought to the living room
Through TV's window the death and gloom
That made students throw the "rocks of ages"
And the guardsmen throw the lethal lead,
Leaving nine kids wounded and four kids dead.

"It's just not right, Arthur, in this nation,
That innocent citizens too must die!
What took place in this awful confrontation
Shouts that the 'Rule of Law' is a lie."
    "Come on now, Liz, this is overreaction.
That mob represents the radical faction
That's growing like cancer in this land.
I don't see why you can't understand.
Those hippies knew just what they were doing.
I'll admit it's too bad that anyone died,
But America's patience is being tried.
When anyone acts, there will be ensuing
Reaction. And that's just what happened here.
It's this Leftist crap that we have to fear."

"It's like you, Arthur, to show such malice
And pretend that it's down to politics.
In truth it's just that you are callous
And using your usual verbal tricks."
Edie had finished her princess sketching.
The California Zephyr was stretching
Its length like a snake across the land.
Their quarrel she did not understand.
"Your actual fears are economic.
I know you, Arthur, the money's the thing.
Any threat to your precious wealth would bring
Your favor in all wars—short of atomic."
    "Well, that's a preposterous thing to say!"
Just then the dark of a tunnel held sway.

When they emerged, her parents were quiet.
Edith showed her mother the princess sketch.
There was no more talk of the college riot.
Years later, Edie's art would fetch
Admirers. And she was widely respected
For her paintings, most of which reflected
A troubled soul, but few could guess
The truths of the past she sought to express.
"That's very good, Dear. What did you name her?
What wonderful work—and all done freehand!
She looks like a queen of some great fairyland."
    "She's Princess Edith." But she never became her.
The three settled down for the long night's rest,
And the blood-red sun slipped down the West.

V
2001

"In New York City, there is rubble
And smoke." Daddy said two planes
Exploded—buildings fell—the bubble
Of a quiet morning broke. "What remains
Is worse than a war zone. A scene of terror."
Mummy asked if he was in error.
"My God, it can't be real," she said.
"Hundreds of people crushed and dead."
And Daddy said the number's rising
As searchers find new bodies there.
"There's something toxic in the air.
They're wearing masks. It's not surprising
Since so much structure turned to dust—
The news almost too grave to trust."

What followed was another scuffle
Between her parents over what
The army should do, and their kerfuffle
Was nothing new to Edie, but
She'd had enough and shifted her focus
(Through some mental hocus pocus)
To picture the ending of their trip,
A railroad atlas in her grip.
Their last stop: California. Frisco.
On the colored pages on her lap,
She traced the northern counties. A map
Showed Sacramento, San Francisco,
Then Palo Alto, San Jose.
They'd be there by the end of day.

"Your Uncle Clarence lives in Berkeley,"
Daddy'd told her back at home.
"A den of Lefties," he'd said curtly.
Puzzled, Edie had thought of a poem
She'd read about an all-left-handed
Village in a country that demanded
Everyone to write with their right.
If she lived there, she thought she might
Practice drawing with her other
Hand to flout the unfair law.
She shook her head and rubbed her jaw,
Noting that her father and mother
Had paused their argument to stare
At a giant insect floating there

Outside the window, before it vanished
As quickly as it came. Red-gold,
It looked to be a moth—a banished
Butterfly, lost, eons old,
And larger than a tabby kitten
Edie'd held in a winter mitten
At a Christmas pageant years before.
It was a gold-winged dinosaur
That had no purpose in the present—
A wormhole or a time machine
Had brought it here; what could it mean?—
Not beautiful, but not unpleasant,
Half luna moth, half sparrowhawk,
That Edie wanted to sketch in chalk.

Of San Francisco, Edie thought of
A silhouette of dizzy hills,
Cable cars, and quite a lot of
Tall, thin houses standing still
Beside the Golden Gate. However,
She was fairly sure the city never
Had been a mecca for mutant bugs
Or huge anachronistic slugs.
The shudder-fly they'd seen was native
To scorched Nevadan desert plains
Where Gila monsters waited for rains
Beneath the prickly pears. Creative
As she was, the girl could not have made
Up such a trick as Nature played.

The bright chimera gone, the morning's
Disastrous news came back with force.
Mummy asked if there were warnings—
What made Edie think "divorce"?—
And Daddy sighed, "Yes, there'd been chatter,
The TV said, but only a scatter
Of hard intel the FBI
And CIA could verify."
He'd left for the club car after learning
That every plane was on the ground.
He'd returned soon after, having found
No comfort in the clips of burning
Buildings—Manhattan, the Pentagon—
As their westward trek trailed on and on.

VI
2037

The bullet train to Solstice Station
From San Francisco's transit hub
Was now the fastest in the nation,
Which, the year before, had joined the club
Of countries with no-fly zones, border
To border—a must to maintain order
Since satellites shot down twelve jets
With secret lasers. Then came the bets
On who the culprit was—some sources
Said North Korea and Iran,
While not one guesser named Japan.
Osaka, though, was home to forces
Of global chaos—a hacker team
That vloggers called The Nil Regime.

Not since Denver had E's folks spoken
More than a few clipped comments, but
Something had changed, the silence broken
By Daddy's sudden move to shut
The door to the aisle. When he was seated,
He looked to his wife, to E—defeated
To a degree he'd never reached before.
Prior, he'd come out ready for war,
As threatening as a nuke-tipped missile.
Yet now, at hundreds of miles an hour,
He was sapped of all his firepower.
He said no words but gave a whistle
That started high and swiftly dropped,
Like a rocket falling, until he stopped

Then clapped his hands, a flat concussion
That jarred E and her mother hard.
It seemed to say, "End of discussion.
No other claim should you regard
As true. Our destination's nearing,
And all our hopes are disappearing."
E's phone perked up. She had a text
And wondered what she should do next:
Answer it and risk Dad's ravings,
Or leave it be until their trip
Had finished at the shuttle strip?
(She knew they'd given all their savings
To take a Mars-bound one-way ride.)
Her mother sat, electrified

As though live wires brushed her body,
And E switched off her phone. No friend
Was texting her to chat. Already
She'd sent them her goodbyes. To pretend
She'd see them all again was silly.
In months she'd be on hilly, chilly,
Rust-hued-dust-storm-two-moon Mars,
A pioneer among the stars.
And they'd be left—her schoolmates, neighbors—
Spinning on a worsening Earth;
Too poor to leave, too young to birth
Another world, despite their labors,
With murder-drones above the clouds
And rancor in the gathering crowds.

The triple-glass that separated
In from Out reflected back
Their small compartment. Aggravated,
E could see zilch beyond the track.
The hurtling train car held a note of
Sitting in a locomotive
Ages ago, nine lives ago,
In an antiquated dress, chapeau,
And ankle boots with tight black laces.
Then, flashing forward, other Es
Named Edith, Edie—binaries
From different times, divergent places;
But unlike a case of déjà vu,
E could read their memories, too.

When Solstice Station, sprawling, gleaming,
Hailed to slow the bullet train,
E, so wide awake that dreaming
Fled farther, farther from her brain,
Began to hum a Grieg sonata
Her father played at a sailing regatta
When she—this she—was very young.
She puffed her cheeks, stuck out her tongue,
And, like a toddler, started crying
For every Edith she had been.
Mother/Liz forgave her own sin,
Her abstract love solidifying,
As she stretched her arms to clutch her child...
And, elsewhere, other Ediths smiled.

Notes on Forms

I "The Exorcised Lyric, 1901"
A Double Crown of Sonnets in Various Forms
Collaboration by Steven Withrow and Frank Coffman

II Twenty Poems by Steven Withrow

NOTE: Steven Withrow's "Caged Animals," "The Burning Man," and "A Means of Summoning" first appeared in *Spectral Realms #14*.

Notes on Forms (cont.)

III Twenty Poems by Frank Coffman

42 "The Line" is an irregular sonnet.

43 "He Who Waits" is an Italian Sonnet.

44 "Xenomnesia" is English Sonnet.

45 "The Valdemar Effect" is an English Sonnet.

47 "The Blue Holes of Andros" is a nonce form.

49 "Year's End" uses the pattern of Clark Ashton Smith's poem, "The End of Autumn."*

50 "Beyond The Veil" is an irregular sonnet.

51 "Agon" is a Bowlesian/Australian Sonnet*

53 "Ouroboros" is in two Couplet Sonnets.

54 "Submission: Never Total" is an English Sonnet.

55 "Micro-Organisms" is a Ballad Sonnet.*

56 "Lycan" uses the pattern of Clark Ashton Smith's poem, "Zothique."*

58 "Words on Ghastly Vellum Writ" — uses two English Sonnets.

59 "Captain Gruchy's Ghost" is a short sequence of illegular sonnets

62 "Past Tense" is a Coffman Sonnet, Type 5*

63 "As Summer Turns to Autumn" is a Latvian Daina Sonnet*

64 "Negative Space" is a Couplet Sonnet

65 "Dawn of the Night" is a Korean Kasa Sonnet*

66 "Halloween/Samhain" uses tetrameter Sicilian Quatrains (ABAB)

68 "La Villa Infestada" is a sequence of Stornello Sonnets*

IV "Toward Solstice Station"
is a collaboration in *Onegin*-Pushkin Sonnets
by Steven Withrow and Frank Coffman

NOTE: Frank Coffman's poetic forms marked with an asterisk are presented in detailed definitions and descriptions at the following web page: http://www.frankcoffman.net/TEL/forms.html

COLOPHON

The Face used for the text—
both poetry and prose sections—is
Adobe Caslon Pro
in various sizes of both Roman and *Italic* fonts

Major division Titles
are set in William Morris' "Golden Type"
in various sizes and weights.
Morris designed this face and used it in
several publications from his Kelmscott Press.

THE COVER
AND INTERIOR MAIN TITLES
ARE SET IN ORBE PRO